Story by

After Dark

Pictures by Susan Varley

LITTLE
MAMMOTH

It's after dark,
time for bed.
Mum will give you a kiss and a hug
and wish you sweet dreams.

Mum's going out to buy some food.
She's been working all day and couldn't find time.
She won't be long, she'll be home soon
(and Pete's in the cellar, fixing his bike.
He'll look after you).

It's after dark;
time to go to sleep.
Time to close your eyes.
Mum will be back soon.

Mum's gone out to buy some food.
She's stopped at the late-night shop for fruit and
vegetables: peas and potatoes, bananas and pears,
(and Pete's in the cellar, fixing his bike).

It's after dark,
time to be sleeping and dreaming.
Why are you sitting up in bed?
Why are your eyes wide open?
Mum will be back soon.

Mum's in the shop buying lots of things:
bread and milk and a bar of chocolate for you,
(and a packet of chewing gum for Pete,
who's down in the cellar fixing his bike).

It's long after dark:
time to be dreaming dreams.
Why are you sitting at the top of the stairs?
Mum will be back soon.

Mum's at the cinema looking at what's on,
smelling the smell of popcorn
and remembering when she was a girl
(while Pete's in the cellar, fixing his bike).

It's after dark,
time to be fast asleep.
Why are you halfway down the stairs?
Mum will be home soon.

Mum's walking past a pub,
lit up with coloured lights.
The music drifts into the street,
(and Pete's in the cellar, fixing his bike).

It's after dark:
time to be warm and fast asleep.
What are you doing at the foot of the stairs?
Mum will be home soon.

Mum's coming home through the dark night streets.
The houses are all lit up.
People are getting ready for dinner.
(One of them isn't thinking about dinner at all,
she's talking on the phone).

It's long, long after dark:
time for you to be fast asleep in bed.
Why are you opening the front door?
Mum will be home soon.

Mum's walking home
through the bright black streets.
An aeroplane flies across the moon.
On a bench by the church
an old couple are holding hands,
(and Pete's in the cellar, fixing his bike).

It's after dark.
Long past your bedtime.
"What are you doing, sitting on the doorstep?"

"I'm waiting for Mum."

First published in Great Britain 1984 by Andersen Press Ltd
Magnet paperback edition published 1986 by Methuen Children's Books Ltd
Published 1989 by Little Mammoth, an imprint of Mandarin Paperbacks
Mandarin is an imprint of the Octopus Publishing Group
Text copyright © 1984 Louis Baum: Illustrations copyright © 1984 Susan Varley
Printed in Great Britain by Scotprint Ltd, Musselburgh   ISBN 0 7497 0172 2